Otto Shares a Hug and a Kiss

written and illustrated

by

Kathleen Morey

kid·love

unlimited

Costa Mesa
California

Published by
kid-love unlimited
1649 D. Iowa Street
Costa Mesa, California
92626

Manufactured in the United States of America

Hoover Printing and Lithography, Inc.
Costa Mesa, California

Calligraphic text by Anita Egan Healy
Newport Beach, California

Second Printing

Library of Congress catalog number 83-80189

Morey, Kathleen
Otto Shares a Hug and a Kiss

Summary: Recounts in rhyme the wonder of a hug and a kiss:
the joy of giving and the thrill of receiving.
I. Morey, Kathleen. II. Title.

ISBN 0-912249-00-5

Hugs and Kisses
all your days
to
Maryon and Truman,
my mom and dad.

P.S. thanks for the red, dad! ♥

If something's *amiss*
and I'm feeling blue,
a hug and a kiss
always help me through.

I throw o·p·e·n my arms
and I pucker my lips
as I wait for the joy
of a hug and a kiss.

If I'm racing along

and

end

up

AGH!!!

UPSIDE DOWN

a hug and a kiss

feel better than bliss.

I throw o·p·e·n my arms
and I pucker my lips;
my mom holds me tight
in a hug and a kiss.

If my tricycle slides

far behind as I ride,

I stay there and wish
for a hug and a kiss.

I throw o·p·e·n my arms
and I pucker my lips;
as my dad picks me up
in a hug and a kiss.

If I slam shut the door
forgetting my finger,
a hug and a kiss
won't let the hurt linger.

And late at night
when it's dark in the hall,
a hug and a kiss
take care of it all.

But that's not all...

Life is not easy
when you're 2, 3, or 4;
but a hug and a kiss
help you on as before.

It matters not
if you're 5 or you're 8;
a hug and a kiss
are always first rate.

As a matter of fact,
believe it or not,
my mom and my dad
hug and kiss quite a lot.

Whatever your age
if something's am*iss*,
treat yourself
to a hug and a kiss.

Throw o·p·e·n your arms
and *pucker* your lips;

grab who's beside you

in a hug and a kiss.

And when everything's fine
and you don't really need it,
GIVE a hug and a kiss;
you just won't believe it.

♥

Throw o·p·e·n your arms
and pucker your lips;

love and be loved

with a hug and a kiss.

The end

ABOUT THE AUTHOR

Inspired by the magic of her son, Kathleen Morey created Otto, the character who is Out To Teach Optimism.

Born in Minneapolis, Morey grew up in Los Angeles where she received her degree in English from Mt. St. Mary's College. Her frustrations in finding the illustrator to translate her concept of Otto led Morey to enroll in a local cartooning course where Otto became a reality; his dog, Tik, soon came rushing out of her pen to make himself known.

Otto Shares a Hug and a Kiss is the first of Morey's series of books in which Otto shares the ultimate good that is in every feeling a child has.

Morey and family live in Newport Beach, California.